W9-AVO-721

Jr
This book belongs to

THE LITTLE ALIEN

ATTACK OF THE BAD TOOTH FAIRY

Story
Jason Quinn

Illustration, Letters and Design
Rajesh Nagulakonda

Editing
Sourav Dutta

Desktop Publishing
Bhavnath Chaudhary

Mission Statement

To entertain and educate young minds by creating unique illustrated books that recount stories of human values, arouse curiosity in the world around us, and inspire with tales of great deeds of unforgettable people.

Published by Kalyani Navyug Media Pvt Ltd
101 C, Shiv House, Hari Nagar Ashram,
New Delhi 110014, India

ISBN: 978-93-81182-13-0

Printed in India

ATTACK OF THE BAD TOOTH FAIRY

KALYANI NAVYUG MEDIA PVT LTD

Our story begins in a house on the edge of town,
on a Sunday night when the moon is round.
When the moon is full and round and bright,
when all good children have said good night.
zzZ...

Little Lily is dreaming of things that are fun, not scary.
She's dreaming about the Good Tooth Fairy.
She lost a tooth at school and so,
she put it under her pillow.
The fairy may swap her tooth for money,
she may stop and play, that would be funny.

Look! Is that the fairy at the window?
It's hard to tell, but I don't think so.
It looks too big and it looks too lumpy,
it looks too large, and stumpy, and bumpy.

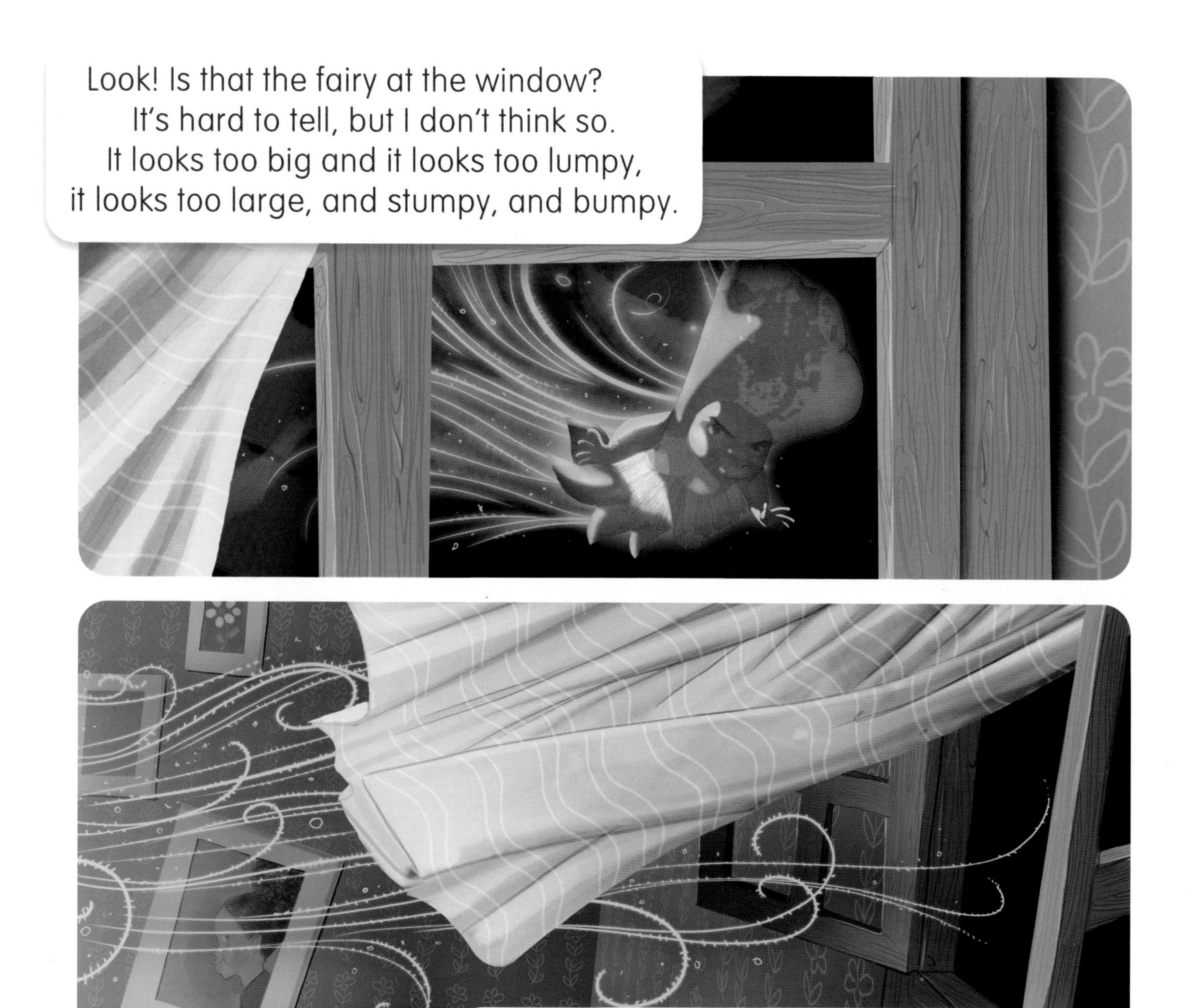

The window is open and in comes a smell.
It stinks of old fish and feet and armpits as well.
It smells of boiled rubbish, it reeks of dead rat.
It smells of something sicked up by a cat.

Oh dear, oh no! It's worse than we thought!
It's the Bad Tooth Fairy, she isn't too tall, she is quite short.
She's smelly, and nasty, and wicked, and mean.
She's the meanest creature you ever have seen.
I'm here on a mission, I'm here on a job,
I'm a tooth snatching, tooth stealing,
tooth grabbing slob!

The Bad Tooth Fairy finds Lily's tooth,
it's under her pillow, it's not on the roof.

Now I must be on my way,
more teeth to steal, so I
can't stay.

But the next morning Lily
didn't find any money.
This isn't fair!
This isn't funny!

Next day, at school, Lily soon found she was not alone,
the Tooth Fairy had been to lots of homes,
She had taken their teeth but not left any cash.
She had left nothing at all but the smell of old trash.
The Tooth Fairy's a thief, a rotten old cheat.
She took my tooth and left nothing, not even a treat.

She took my tooth too, and
Jim's and Rita's,
and Bobby's and Anna's and
Pedro's and Peter's.
She stole my dog's teeth, now
he has to eat soup,
he can't eat solids, just gloopy
old gloop.
There's no need to cry, there's no need to yelp.
My friend Janet can give us some help.
She's used to the strange, the bad, and the wrong,
she could help us, it won't take her long.

Look! In the sky is the girl from another planet!
It's Bob's best friend, her name is Janet.
Her pet cat Hiss is with her too.
They've come to help, of course it's true.
Tell me friends, what is the problem?
We love puzzles and we always solve them.

I know who did this; I know who's to blame.
The Bad Tooth Fairy is her name!
She's wanted across the universe,
for stealing teeth and things much worse.
We'll stop her crimes, we'll make her pay!
Let's go and see her right away!
She lives on the far side of the sun,
we had better hurry, we'd better run!
Let's go! Let's go!
Let's go!
Come on everyone,
don't say no!

Look at the gang as they race through space.
Look up ahead, what's that strange place?
It's a world that looks like a big sharp fang.
That's where the Bad Tooth Fairy likes to hang.
Okay, gang, we're nearly there,
but do be careful, do take care.
The Bad Tooth Fairy doesn't like guests,
she doesn't like children, she thinks they're pests.

Follow me, but do beware,
danger is waiting everywhere.
Be quiet as a kitten or
quiet as a mouse,
as we reach the Bad
Tooth Fairy's house.

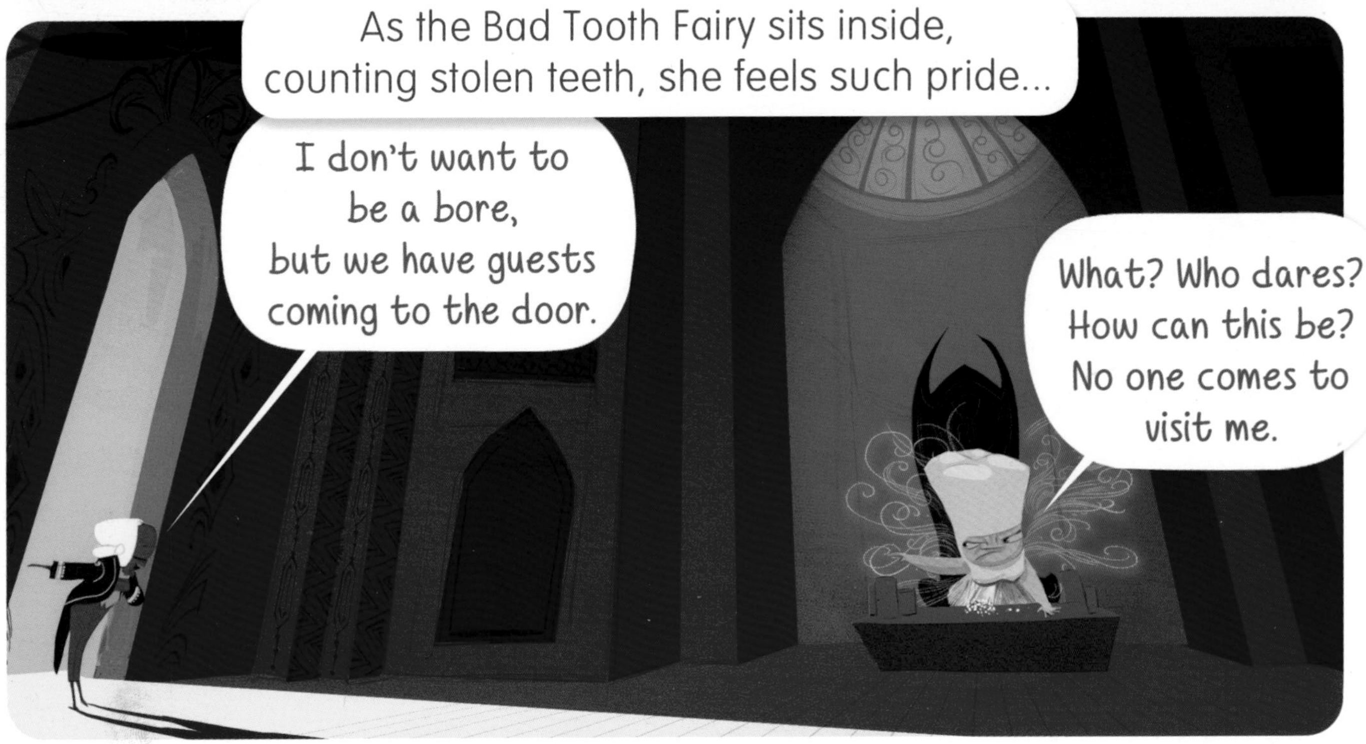
As the Bad Tooth Fairy sits inside,
counting stolen teeth, she feels such pride...
I don't want to
be a bore,
but we have guests
coming to the door.
What? Who dares?
How can this be?
No one comes to
visit me.

Children? Here? Right here today?
I think it's time to make them pay,
for coming here uninvited,
and running around all so excited!

I'll steal their teeth and pull their hair,
and if they cry, well I won't care,
because I'm nasty, mean and bad,
and I love making people sad!

I'll tie you all up in a dirty old sack,
but first get ready for a...
PLAQUE ATTACK!

The Bad Tooth Fairy swoops down to attack,
she attacks from the front, she attacks from the back.
With a BIFF and a POW and a WHAM and a WHACK,
she catches Bob and Lily and a boy called Jack.

The Little Alien leaves her friends behind.
What's going on? Has she lost her mind?
She's flying away from the Bad Tooth Fairy,
does she really find her all that scary?
Is she a coward? Is she a chicken?
Or is she not well? Is she starting to sicken?
Or is it all part of a brilliant plan?
If we read on we might understand.

But for the moment, we'll just have to wait,
and travel inside the Bad Tooth Fairy's gate,
where all our friends, our pals, our mates,
are stuck like pudding on a plate.
Welcome prisoners, to my hall,
I won't steal one tooth, I'll take them all.
And don't think of escape, don't be clever,
you're stuck with me forever and ever.

The friends begin to argue and fight,
they know it's wrong, it isn't right,
but they're scared and helpless, you'd feel the same.
They all want somebody to blame.
Bob's friend got us into this mess,
Bob and Janet caused this stress!

It's not fair
blaming me for this.
Oh come back, Janet,
come back, Hiss!

Oh, dear, oh dear, is my guest in tears?
Is he unhappy, shall I pull his ears?
Shall I pinch his cheek and twist his nose,
shall I jump up and down on his poor little toes?
Yes, oh, yes, do all
these things,
And slap his face
until it stings,.
Listen can you hear that sound?
It's in the air and all around.
It sounds like little fluttering wings,
it sounds like bees, or birds, and flying things.

I'll give you one chance to surrender,
release my friends, you big pretender!
Do it now or face big trouble,
I'll turn your castle into rubble.

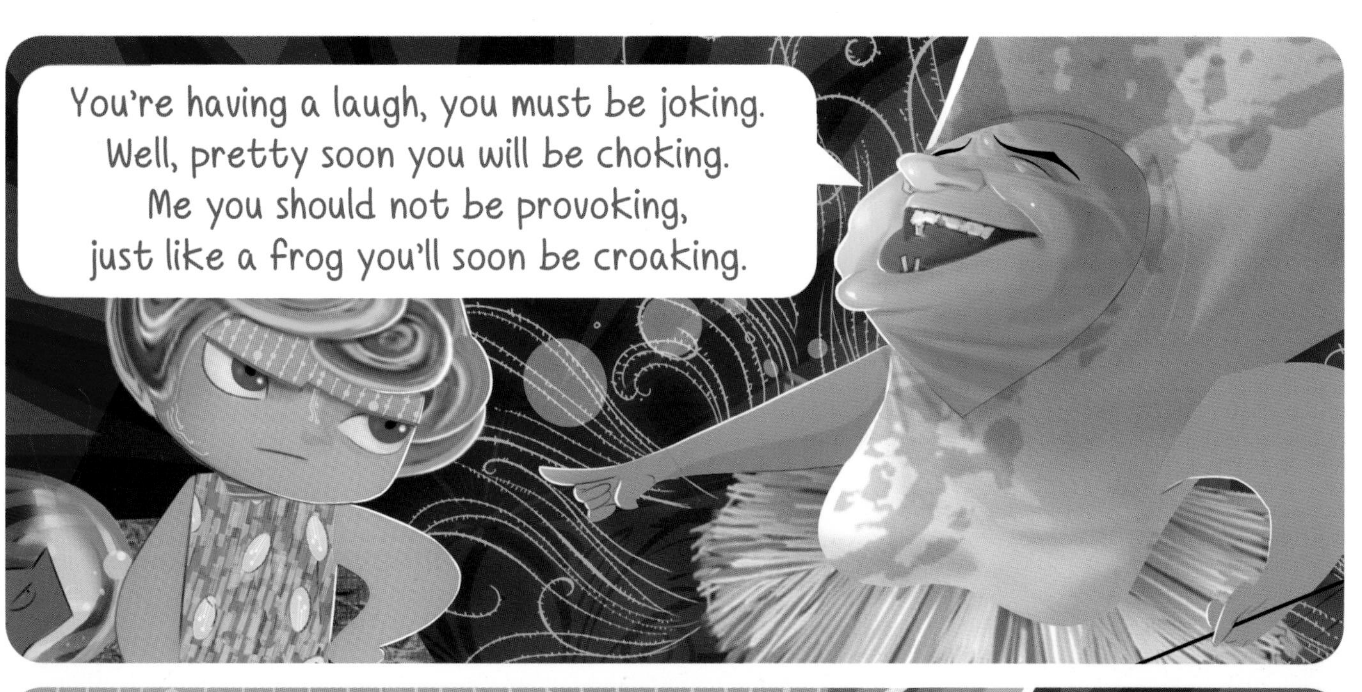
You're having a laugh, you must be joking.
Well, pretty soon you will be choking.
Me you should not be provoking,
just like a frog you'll soon be croaking.

You'll be so sorry, you'll
wish you listened.
But you've had your
chance, you rotten villain.

PHWWWWWEEEEEEP

As Janet whistles long and loud,
Good Tooth Fairies burst from the clouds.
They want to set the children free
and punish that wicked Bad Tooth Fairy.
Don't worry kids, you'll
be coming with us.
Don't worry about
missing your next bus.

But first we'll deal with
the Bad Tooth Fairy,
we're good but we too
can be scary.
We've come to take
her in her den,
she won't steal your
teeth ever again.

You can care for your teeth in three easy stages. They're easy to learn, they don't take ages.

Who cares about your steps and stages? I'll crush you all within these pages. What are your stages and your steps? Something stupid I suspect.

Step one for perfect dental care,
brush with toothpaste, everywhere.
A good toothpaste can really clean
stains that are stubborn and nasty and mean.

The Bad Tooth Fairy gets it in the face,
she's covered in toothpaste, what a disgrace.
With a splat and a squish and a splish and a splash,
the toothpaste hits her in a flash.

Step Two now, listen to the Boss,
it's time to use your dental floss.
MMMPH. . .
The Bad Tooth Fairy is bound up tight,
with super floss, yes floss, that's right.
She's tied so tight, she can't get free.
There's no way out that she can see.

Now comes step three, so swish and splosh,
let's rinse things off with some **mouthwash**.

Okay, okay, you have your goal,
I'll pay these kids money for the teeth I stole.

With the Bad Tooth Fairy wet and beaten,
now this story we can sweeten.
Bob and his friends we have to free,
let's do it on the count of three.
zzzZAAAAP!
Don't panic, don't worry, stay calm please,
this may tickle you around your knees.
It will soon be over can't you see?
You'll all be coming home with me.

At last they're free to scratch and itch,
to stretch their arms and legs like this,
to run and hop and skip and jump,
at last they're free to leave this dump.
Bob's friend saved us, I knew she would! Being free, it feels so good!

Wait, please wait! Before we leave, the Bad Tooth Fairy has gifts for you, I believe.

For every tooth the Tooth Fairy stole,
she has to pay a bag of gold.
She isn't happy with the deal,
it makes her want to shout and squeal.

Look, Bob! Look, we're rich! We're we rich! I'll buy a car or a boat, I don't know which.
You could get both, yes, I've been told, you can buy a lot with a bag of gold.
12
9
3
6

It's time to go, I do believe,
let's say goodbye before we leave.
We'll meet again, someday soon,
here, or at home, or on the moon.
Goodbye, take care!
Have fun flying through the air!

Go, just go, quick, go, get lost!
I wish our paths had never crossed!
I've lost a fortune, it's just not fair,
so go, just go, get out of my hair!

Look! We're entering our solar system,
but listen to this piece of wisdom,
even if it seems like fun,
never look closely at the sun.
We're going super fast so hold tight, please,
we'll be home before you can blink or sneeze.

Well, our trip was really cool, but now we're back, it's time for school.
Children, children! Come on, you're late! Class is starting, don't make me wait.

Your friend Janet
is lots of fun,
where do you think
it is she's gone?
She goes to school
up on the moon.
Don't worry, I'm sure we'll
see her again quite soon.

Children, you're in class, so please don't chatter,
wait until later if you want a natter.
Today, we'll learn about tooth care,
so open your books and sit in your chairs.

Meanwhile, very very far away,
Janet is taking a holiday.
Come on Hiss
let's go faster,
I'm feeling hungry, do
you feel like pasta?
12
3
6
9

Space spaghetti would be nice, it tastes so good with moon dust spice.

The Bad Tooth Fairy has learned her lesson,
with your teeth she won't be messing.
But to keep your teeth healthy follow the plan,
just brush, floss and mouthwash twice a day if you can.

Imagine your best friend comes from another world.
He could be a boy, or she could be a girl.
You could explore space every day,
you could splash around in the Milky Way.
You could visit a planet made out of stinky cheese,
you could go anywhere, wherever you please.
Come with us, up into the sky,
let your imagination really fly!

Jr
CAMPFIRE®
www.campfire.co.in

Jason Quinn
Rajesh Nagulakonda
THE LITTLE
ALIEN
Jr
CAMPFIRE®
A journey of imagination

OTHER TITLES FROM CAMPFIRE JUNIOR

Little Ganesha is always getting up to mischief and this is your chance to join him and his family for two fun-filled adventures that will stay with you forever!

We all love animals and magical talking animals are the best of the lot. Goldilocks and the Three Bears, the Three Little Pigs, and the Frog Prince are all waiting for you in the village of Ever-After, ready to excite you with brand new versions of their timeless bed-time stories.